hero cape

cindy henkelman

For more information, herocape.ca.

Published in October, 2025

Developmental Editor - Anna Bierhaus
Copy Editor - Kelsey Mitchener
Cover Artist - John Roberts
Book Design - Veronica Scott

ISBN 978-1-7383963-0-6 (paperback)
ISBN 978-1-7383963-2-0 (ebook)

To my girl...
I hear you; I see you. And I will always love you.
To Katherine, my light...
I can now look in the mirror,
and see beauty and courage in the girl
staring back at me.

INTO THE LION'S MOUTH

Into the Lion's mouth they say...
Why would you go down to the dock?
To sit at the water's edge.
All by yourself.
So far away.
Letting the darkness swallow you whole.
The wind so loud, your footsteps...silent in the sand...

Into the Lion's mouth they say...
How dare you feel the need for solitude.
How dare you let the quiet beckon you.
How dare you seek to gaze at the stars.
So far away.
On that lonely dock.
Letting the night breeze call out to you...

Into the Lion's mouth they say...
The voices playing over and over in my mind.
Scolding, scathing words.
But it's his voice that stands out.
You asked for this.
You wanted this.
Don't play coy with me...

Into the Lion's mouth they say...
A world too cruel for the naïve.

For someone like me.
Curious, playful, intrigued.
Stalked by the cowardly hyena.
Attacked by the cowardly hyrax.
Damaging every fibre of my being...

Into the Lion's mouth they say...
A scar too deep to share.
An irreparable wound.
Living a life of hurt.
Hurt by life itself.
Not trusting.
Just existing.

Into the Lion's mouth they say...
The scar, a reminder of a lifetime ago.
But no more guilt.
No more shame.
The wind dies down.
The voices grow quiet.
Now it's only my voice I hear...

Into the Lion's mouth they say
To that I say...

I AM THE LION

Introduction

This isn't your typical story. Where the good guy wins. Where all the loose ends are tied together by the time you get to the last chapter. No, this isn't that kind of story. There are two stories told here, one equally as important as the other. Two stories about two very different women.

Baby A

...

I'm a twin. Yes, that is seriously the only interesting fact about me. We were born almost two months prematurely. I came out first, weighing two pounds; my identical twin, Meredith, weighing a whopping three pounds. I stayed in the incubator fighting for my life for an extra month, but apparently I was the first to lift my head up. The doctor told my mother that Baby A was strong. A fighter. And he had no doubt she'd survive. And survive I did. This strength was the same strength I needed twenty years later...

At the point in my life where I'll begin my story, I had been working at a café for about two years. I also played on a women's soccer team with Meredith. This was really the extent of my day-to-day life. I didn't have much else going on for me.

I will now fast-forward to the day that led to the night I am still trying to forget. There's really no point to speak in any more detail of the life I had before this. It seems irrelevant.

Ordinary Day

···

The day was like any other day for me. The café was busy on a Friday during the lunch hour rush, like always. Its location is conveniently placed amongst a street full of shops and businesses, its patrons consisting of regulars who worked close by, as well as random people experiencing the café for the first time. It has a cozy, friendly feel to it, the outside made of traditional red brick. Even its name is inviting: Dog Dayz Cafe. Inside, an antique oak shelf lines the left wall, full of books and board games that are available for anyone's use. Each table is a different style, purposely done to give the space an eclectic look. Some are made of wood, others of metal. Some are round; others are square or rectangular in shape. Even the chairs are different and random, reflecting the variety and uniqueness of the customers who visited each day. At the center of it all is a two-way red brick fireplace that reaches the ceiling, with brown leather couches on either side that were almost always occupied. The back wall was where the action was, with employees busy serving customers their lunch orders, the kitchen just behind it, accessed through two swinging red doors. From 6 a.m. to 2 p.m. Monday to Friday, I was here, baking in the morning, then cleaning tables and serving customers for the lunch hour until my shift was done.

I gazed out the window at the beautiful sunny day with hardly a cloud or breeze to offer any relief from the heat. The honking of a car horn, most likely from an impatient driver, startled me back to reality. Although I did not particularly enjoy work, I was thankful to be inside this air-conditioned space during this heat wave that had now been going on for over a week, with no end in sight.

"Sydney, can you close the blinds, please?"

My manager Lydia's voice could be heard across the entire café. She's a short, loud, robust woman who you didn't question. You just obeyed. That was her quiet voice. Her loud voice was the one you didn't want to hear.

So, I did just as she asked. I closed the blinds a bit, noticing the sunlight was in fact bothering the customers. I continued cleaning the tables as customers left, trying to avoid making eye contact with anyone. Having to talk to someone, especially a stranger, scared me. I always felt awkward, even with people I knew. But as much as I avoided people, I found them fascinating. People from all walks of life, coming in for a sandwich, soup, coffee, or dessert. Some ate feverishly, trying to get back to where they had to be. Sitting by themselves. Some sat in groups. Telling stories. Laughing and taking the time to enjoy each other's company. I was always curious about the life each person had outside these walls. *Where are they off to? Do they have important jobs? People to meet? Do they have kids? What kind of families do they come from?* This all fascinated me. I'd imagine what they'd be rushing off to. Surely somewhere more important than where I had to go. As I mentioned previously, my daily life consisted of working and playing soccer—then going home to my one-bedroom apartment in the north end of the city. That was really all I did. My sister's constant attempts to get me to do anything else I mostly ignored.

On this day, my thoughts were a bit negative, which really wasn't unusual, per se. I had a party to go to that night. Our women's soccer team had organized it with the men's team: a party at a lake that was just twenty minutes southwest of town. A party I was dreading to go to. The mere thought of it put me in a mood. I continued to clean off the now empty tables in the café as the lunch hour came to an end. Everyone had left but an older couple, who remained at a table by the front window. They were drinking their coffees and chuckling over something said in the deep conversation they were having. *She is aging well*, I thought. The white and dark streaks of her short hairstyle shone under the sun. It looked like a fresh cut, as if she had just come from the salon. Even the little wrinkles I noticed around her mouth when she smiled looked beautiful on her. *She must smile often*, I thought to myself. She was glowing. The gentleman sitting across from her hadn't aged as well, but he still had a handsome, wise look about him. His hair was completely white, but his slightly bushy eyebrows were still quite dark. Their hands were interlocked as they continued with their conversation, oblivious to the fact that I was staring at them with a look of envy. As I finally looked away, I thought to myself, *will I ever find someone to laugh with? Someone who understands me? Someone who finds me attractive, even on my worst days?* Because I thought of myself as anything but attractive. Looking in the mirror was a difficult task in itself. Not only did I avoid making eye contact with people in general, but I also avoided looking at the girl staring back at me. The plain-looking, brown-eyed girl. The girl with the straight, shoulder-length, boring brown hair, which was either pulled tight into a ponytail or hidden under a ball cap. The five-feet-four slender-built girl with the somewhat long, pointed nose. The girl with the small but noticeable gap between her two front teeth. The girl who rarely smiled. The girl I hated being.

Just then two police officers walked in, the bell on the door startling me back to reality. I hadn't realized I had zoned out—something I tend to do quite often. The first officer was an older male, possibly in his late fifties, who seemed like the one in charge. I noticed on his uniform that he had three white stripes at the shoulders. He had a weary look on his face. A tired and exhausted look. The stubble on his face and dishevelled salt-and-pepper hair hinted at possibly a long day or week for him. The other police officer was a younger female. Possibly in her late twenties or early to mid thirties? It was hard to tell her age. I noticed she had only the one stripe on her uniform. She had brown hair like mine, pulled up in a tight bun. She had it pulled so tight that it seemed to pull at her face as well. She gave me a smile as she walked by. Immediately I felt my face turn hot and I started blushing with embarrassment. For no apparent reason. But that's what I did. That's what I always did. I never felt important enough for anyone to give me a smile. Or, heaven forbid, to make conversation with me. So, I put my head down and continued to clean off the tables. The two police officers ordered their cinnamon buns and coffees to go. As they walked out, the woman gave me another friendly smile. At this point I felt a tinge of jealousy. That's how I'd describe what I felt at that precise moment. Here I was cleaning dirty plates off tables, and this woman was leaving, with a much more important job to do. I felt even smaller in this big world of much more important people. People who made a difference. What difference was I making? I was a nobody. Destined always to be a nobody. I felt invisible. *Why do I have to be so shy?*

I finished cleaning up, making sure every little crumb or coffee stain vanished off the tables and chairs. Then I wiped them down again, for good measure. Lydia wasn't too fond of my attention to detail when it came to cleaning. There were more important things to tend to in her opinion. But I couldn't help myself. I was a bit of a perfectionist. When I put effort into a task, I was all in. Almost to the point of having OCD. Especially when it came to cleaning. My apartment and car reflected this: spotless, almost always. In fact, I couldn't leave my apartment unless everything was perfectly in place. I probably washed my car at least twice a week, if not more. This obsession with being clean I inherited from my mother, without a doubt. A lot of my childhood included memories of my mother's constant cleaning, which seemed to occupy most of her time when she wasn't working. This compulsive habit of hers rubbed off on me, while her talent at cooking most definitely did not. *A shame*, I thought to myself.

With this last thought, I walked to the back of the café to hang up my apron. I smiled meekly at my coworkers, looked at the ground, and quickly shuffled my feet out the back entrance. I never stayed to make conversation. I had no conversation to make. The girls were used to this. Me sneaking in, doing my shift, and then quickly sneaking out. Like I was never there. A ghost of a person.

As I walked to my car I noticed Laurel, one of the older ladies, taking her smoke break by the back door. She was the soup lady. She made all the soups from scratch. And she took pride in it. I liked Laurel. Maybe because she was older. I had trouble talking to the younger girls around my age. I never felt cool enough. But Laurel was different. She was a tall, lanky older woman, maybe in her late sixties. I never asked her age, never really thought it that important. I just knew by looking at her that she had worked hard her whole life. Her fiery, short red hair could possibly hint at her being the stereotypical temperamental redheaded woman. She was nothing of the sort. She was a kind and patient woman, with a soothing voice and calm demeanour. I found conversing with her took no effort. She was the one person I did try to speak to at work.

As I opened my car door after struggling to unlock it, I turned and said, "See you, Laurel. Have a good day. I'll see you on Monday."

She quickly looked up with a smile on her face and nodded at me in response, as she took another drag of her cigarette. I climbed into my clean, little 1988 red Honda Civic hatchback, closed the door, and felt instant relief. It was a barrier from the outside world, the metal frame providing me a much-needed safe zone, where I could scream, cry, or just sit in complete silence if I chose to do so. Slowly pulling out of the parking lot, I headed to my little spotless apartment. The drive took about thirty minutes—time I cherished.

Safe Zone

...

I pulled into the parking lot of my apartment complex at around 2:25 p.m., traffic surprisingly lighter than usual. The place I called home for the time being was situated in a derelict neighbourhood, not short on crime. The only beautiful things about the neighbourhood were the massive maple trees that lined the pothole-ridden street. It was an older six-storey building, the siding an ugly green colour that had you believe the building was fighting some sort of illness. At least this is what I envisioned looking at the old structure. It was a place I could afford, though. Slim pickings earning a wage at a café. As I got out of my car and walked through the main entrance, I sighed, having to climb the stairs to the fourth floor. My legs felt heavy and tired. The elevator had been out of service for a month now, with no sign of it getting repaired any time soon. As I approached the door to my apartment, I noticed Miss Landon had her hands full of groceries as she tried wiggling her key in the keyhole to no avail. I quickly walked over and grabbed her grocery bags from her so she could open the door.

"Why thank you, Sydney. I appreciate your help! So, what exciting plans on this gorgeous Friday does a beautiful young girl like yourself have in store?"

I blushed at this compliment, knowing full well she was just being the friendly and kind Dorothy I'd come to know and love. She was a plump, middle-aged woman. Blond, blue eyed, with a perfectly round face and a cute button nose I only dreamed of having. I could tell she used to be a looker. Somewhere along the way she let herself go. Life can do that to someone, I suppose. She never married or had children of her own, a fate I was sure I was destined for. But she always made me feel safe, seen, and heard. She was the only person I felt comfortable enough to confide in. My overly strict and protective parents were not the ones to talk about feelings or anything remotely personal or emotional. Neither was my sister. I only talked to her about superficial things. Anything deeper than that and I found her to get awkward and uncomfortable. I spared putting her in a position that made her feel this way. So Dorothy was my person.

I grunted and told her I had a party to go to at the lake close to town.

With this she squealed with excitement, "Maybe you'll meet a boy! How fun! Wait, let me give you some of my booze to take with you!"

I politely declined, as I never drank. It wasn't my scene. She knew this. Maybe she was hoping this one time I'd be more adventurous, but I liked to have my wits about me. And to be honest, I got satisfaction out of seeing people make fools of themselves. Something about it gave me a sense that others weren't perfect either. Dorothy, however, liked to drink. Quite often, in fact. It was on those nights that I had any chance of beating her at crib. We usually played crib on Friday nights. Today was Friday...

"Dorothy. How about I stay home and we play some crib? I really don't feel like going out tonight. This heat has me wiped out."

She emphatically replied, "Nonsense! You are going out! You are not wasting a chance to hang out with people your own age. And how are you ever supposed to meet a guy, playing crib with me every Friday night? Plus, I'm going to visit my parents for the weekend."

Not the response I was hoping for.

I rolled my eyes at her. "Fine. But it's going to be lame."

I turned and walked across the hall to my apartment. As I opened my door, Dorothy yelled a bit too loud for my liking, "Have a blast tonight! And maybe try and lose your virginity?!"

I wasn't sure if this was a question or a statement. Regardless, I closed the door behind me and leaned against it, letting out a long sigh, glad to be in another safe zone of mine.

Destiny?

I walked straight to my bedroom and got undressed, putting on my white Blink-182 T-shirt my sister had bought me when she saw them in concert the summer before. I always did this as soon as I got home: I put on something comfortable. It was a habit. And not going out very often was probably why I got used to doing this. Today, however, wasn't a usual day for me. I was going out in just a few hours. The countdown was on. But first... a nap, if I were to have any chance of being sociable.

Before I jumped into bed, I noticed my plant. I walked toward my poor, dying plant, which sat on the windowsill, to try to resuscitate it with some water. Thoughts swirled around in my head as I picked up the water pitcher. *Maybe this will be the night. Maybe tonight will be my first kiss. Or more?* Dorothy was right. My romantic life would continue to be nonexistent if I kept choosing to stay home. I stared at my plant for a moment, noticing that more leaves had fallen off. It looked sparser than when I left it that morning. I wondered if it sensed the water close by, tortured by the fact that it could not be reached, as it slowly wilted away to its inevitable death. I flooded the cracked soil and watched in a trance-like state as the water spilled over onto the floor. *Why do I bother? This will be the third plant in two weeks that will meet the same fate*, I thought, annoyed with the mess

I'd made. The heat in my apartment was unbearable. I opened the window and was greeted by a slight warm breeze that caressed my face, offering minimal relief. Better than nothing.

I now jumped into my bed to try to squeeze that nap in, throwing the duvet onto the floor. Meredith would be calling me soon, bugging me to get ready to pick up her and our friend Molly from our parents' house to go to this lake party. I was always the designated driver. It wasn't even a decision that ever had to be made. It was automatic. And I frankly didn't mind. I tried to close my eyes.

The truth of the matter was, I liked a guy. Specifically, I liked Trevor. I hardly knew him, except for the fact that we both were midfielders on our respective soccer teams. We had something in common. That was a start. Had to be destiny, right?

I distinctly remember Trevor smiling at me—more than a couple of times—from his seat at the back of the bus on our way to a tournament, not too long ago. I of course blushed and quickly turned around in my seat to face forward. That entire weekend I avoided him as best as I could. I had no clue what to do with this information anyway. What did a smile mean? Did he like me, too? Most girls would know how to process visual cues. Not me. Nope. But I couldn't ignore the fact that I did feel this nervous excitement whenever I was around him. Just the thought of possibly seeing him tonight put me in a bit of a frenzy.

I was used to all the cool boys liking Meredith. We were technically identical twins. But to me, we were the furthest thing from it. My twin had a different personality than me. Yes, she was shy. But she was normal shy. She didn't avoid social gatherings like I did. She still liked hanging out with friends and going out for drinks. She also had a more positive demeanour about her. And she most definitely did not have my temper. I can recall countless sleepless nights wishing as hard as I could to just be her. I would have done anything to trade places with her. Her facial features were soft. Mine seemed harsher and more distinct. She had a more athletic build—specifically, her calves. This was a result of her walking on her tippy-toes when she was younger. We were different in both personality and physical features, in my opinion, although most people had trouble telling us apart at first glance. So the mere thought of a boy showing interest in me for once, instead of Meredith, made me blush for a second.

I finally closed my eyes and started to drift off to sleep, not knowing my life going forward would drastically change in mere hours. Not knowing that the girl lying so peacefully in her bed would never be the same girl again.

Plain Jane

...

I woke up from my nap to the shrill ringing of my alarm clock, feeling foggy brained and a bit confused. *Maybe I'll call in sick today.* I slammed the snooze button with my hand, knowing full well I wasn't going to be able to fall back asleep anyway. My confusion gave way to the realization that I wasn't getting up to go to work but instead to go to a stupid lake party. I contemplated which was worse and quickly decided the party was less appealing than having to get up for work. I lay there staring at the ceiling, reflecting on the bits and pieces of my dream that I happened to remember. My first kiss. With Trevor. That is what I remembered. I felt a flush come across my face and felt an intense heat throughout my body, the sweat dripping down my chest. It was then that I realized that my entire body was drenched in sweat. From the unbearable heat? Or was it from the not-so-appropriate thoughts I was having at that very moment? Either way, I turned my alarm off and jumped in the shower. The cold water on my face felt good. My shower was a quick one, interrupted by a phone call from my sister, making sure I was on schedule. Heaven forbid we were one minute late for a party I was now dreading going to.

I stood in front of my closet staring at the poor selection of clothing I had to choose from. Mostly athletic wear, hoodies, joggers, and T-shirts. I decided on a pair of cutoff jean shorts and a plain white T-shirt. Plain like myself. No use trying to dress myself up. I was all about comfort. I went in the bathroom and plugged my curling iron in. I wore minimal makeup, mostly because I had little experience with it. Meredith tried to give me a tutorial a few times but to no avail, as I almost always tuned out. My attention span was never very good. So, the only thing I put on my face was mascara. That was it. *Take it or leave it* was the attitude I had on that matter. My face was my face. No amount of makeup would change the boring features of it. And I suppose maybe that was part of the reason boys didn't find me attractive. My sister always took the time to dress nice and put on makeup. She always looked so put together. I'll admit, I was always more than a bit jealous of the fact that my sister had this talent of looking perfect for any type of occasion, while I almost always looked like an afterthought. Because I treated myself that way. I had no one to blame but myself. I decided to unplug the curling iron and instead chose to put on my black New York Yankees ball hat. As always, choosing less effort. I had a lot of hats to choose from. But this one was by far my favourite. I cleaned up, making sure everything was in its perfect place. I grabbed my car keys and headed to my parents' to pick up Meredith and Molly. *Here we go,* I thought. *Let's get this night started. Either the very rare brave version of myself will emerge or the typical shy, boring wallflower will show up.* I was hoping for the brave version for once. I was tired of feeling lonely and longed to be kissed by a boy. To be touched by a boy. Feel what it was like to be sought after and wanted. Wishful thinking, maybe, but it was what got me out the door.

Creature Comforts

...

I drove to the south side of the city to my parents' house. They lived in an older neighbourhood, but it was the definition of suburbia. A quiet neighbourhood with an older population. Heavily treed, with a beautiful park and hill right across the street. As I pulled in front of the familiar yellow bungalow, I looked to the left at the lone park bench sitting on top of the hill. Memories started flooding back of tobogganing with my sister in the winter. Reading countless books on that bench. Rolling down the hill like a log in the summer, getting a rash from the grass. Kicking the soccer ball for hours on end with Meredith, until dark, when Mom would finally yell at us to come in for dinner. Simpler times. A time when life seemed less complicated. I felt safe in that little yellow bungalow. Protected from the intimidating world outside.

Meredith still lived at home. My parents' rule was if we continued with post-secondary education after high school, they would continue supporting us. This meant we could live at home without paying rent. Since I had decided to take a gap year that had turned into two, I had to find work and pay rent. Fine. But if I had to pay rent, I wanted my own place. Their constant badgering and obvious disappointment were all the motivation I needed to take that next step. Meredith had finished her second year of university, on her way to becoming a teacher. Just another thing to add to the list of things I was envious of.

As I got out of my car, I noticed my mother standing at the living room window, watching as I walked up. She did this often. My father, as well. As soon as anyone pulled up, they'd immediately go to the window to see who it was. My parents were the worrying kind of parents. Nosy, as well. They didn't let us do what most teenagers growing up were allowed to do, mostly out of fear of pretty much everything. It explains a lot. I was a rule follower. I just did what my parents told me. As much as I complain about this, I know they raised us the best way they knew how. It was a bit much at times, but I knew it came from a place of love and wanting to protect us from the world. There was frequent yelling; my father's short temper, as well as mine, contributed to most of it. But it was a safe place.

Just then the front door opened, my mother standing there with her apron on and a big smile to greet me. She had short hair that she coloured red most of her life. She is a strong woman, in stature and mind. Working two jobs while somehow raising twins mostly on her own. My father worked up north as an electrician for months at a time. They were the definition of hard workers. I reflected on how much they sacrificed for us. Yes, they absolutely did the best they knew how.

Walking up the steps, I smiled at her appreciatively. "Hi, Mom. What did you whip up for supper tonight?" I asked, eager to eat as I noticed how hungry I was.

She waved me in. "Come eat! There's lots to eat. It's good!"

I chuckled to myself. She has a habit of complimenting her own cooking without even realizing it. She honestly has every right to. Her cooking is amazing. She takes so much pride in every dish she makes, and her passion is seeing people enjoy her meals. I walked in and gave her a big hug. It felt good. We held this hug for longer than usual, both of us obviously missing the other. I could see Meredith and Molly sitting at the table already eating.

Meredith and I had met Molly a year ago when we all joined the same soccer team. She is a few years younger than us, just freshly graduated from high school, with plans on becoming a teacher as well. She was to start university that fall. Molly had a photogenic look to her that I admired. Light brown shoulder-length hair, blue eyes, and a cute little nose. She often complained about her body. What she saw as big boned I saw as strong and athletic.

"Where's Dad?" I asked, scanning the house for him.

My guess was he was either grocery shopping, at the bank, or buying scratch lotto tickets at the gas station. He did this routine almost every day. He had been laid off work temporarily for the last month.

"Who knows where he is," my mother responded with an eye roll.

I then walked to the kitchen and scanned the table at the spread my mom had prepared for us: deep-fried chicken, homemade potato salad, and apple strudel. I pulled up a chair across from Meredith and Molly and sat down.

"Hey, guys."

They both looked up, their laughter from the conversation they just finished trailing off.

"Hey, Syd! Ready for tonight?" Molly asked with obvious excitement that was easily detected in the pitch of her voice.

I usually tried to match her excitement with my responses. A difficult task, as Molly had a naturally bubbly personality. Any excitement in my voice was almost always faked. It was hard work to pretend to always be happy.

"Sure," I replied, too mentally exhausted to put any effort this time in masking my lack of interest.

"How was work?" Meredith asked as she took a bite out of a drumstick.

I wasn't sure how much she really cared about my day. She was already walking away to the fridge to grab a can of ginger ale before I could respond.

"It was fine. Can you grab me a can, too?" I replied.

We sat in silence for a bit as we enjoyed the meal in front of us. I noticed both Meredith and Molly had put makeup on and were wearing cute summer dresses, their hair up in cute messy buns. They looked like maybe they were the twins. I was feeling extra plain now in my tomboy outfit. I was also feeling a little left out...

"Mom, Sydney and I are going to sleep over at Molly's house tonight, after the party," Meredith exclaimed.

We'd never slept at Molly's house, so I was excited to get to that part of the night at least.

"Ok. Just don't drink and drive. And be careful."

"Don't worry, Mom," I said reassuringly. "I'll take care of them like I always do. And I'm not drinking, so I'll be ok to drive."

She had an immediate look of relief on her face as she started cleaning up.

"Thanks so much for dinner!" Molly shouted as we headed to the front door to leave.

I hated that we had to eat and run. I really did miss seeing my mom. It had probably been three weeks since I had visited my parents. I made a point of trying to call them every day, though, which I knew they appreciated. My dad would be sure to remind me if I missed even one day. "I could be dead, for all you know," he would tease morbidly. My dad is always teasing people. He has a sense of humour that takes some time to get used to. In fact, his personality in general takes time to get used to. At six feet two and with his loud, booming voice due to being deaf in one ear, he is not exactly the most approachable person. His short temper doesn't help his demeanour. He also has a habit of rubbing people the wrong way, always too eager to share his viewpoint on certain topics like politics and religion—opinions best kept to yourself in certain situations. For all the gruffness my dad has on the exterior, on the inside, he is just a big teddy bear. Unlike my mom, who holds onto things, my dad never holds grudges and would be the first to apologize. My mother, on the other hand, I have yet to hear apologize for anything she was in the wrong for. Stubborn. The apple didn't fall far from the tree.

"Say hi to Dad for me. And thanks for dinner, Mom."

I gave her one last hug before I bounded down the concrete steps to my car. Molly and Meredith were waiting impatiently for me as they tugged at the door handles. I wished some of their excitement would rub off on me.

Wallflower

...

I drove us to our first stop, the liquor store, before heading out to the lake. The girls went inside to buy what they needed for the night as I waited in the car. No need for me to go in. There were streams of people going in and out of the store, all with smiles on their faces, excited for the start of the weekend. I could see through the store window that Meredith and Molly were busy conversing with two extremely tall, lanky-looking boys as they waited in line to pay for their alcohol. Good on them.

I leaned my head back and closed my eyes for a moment. I visualized Trevor. *Will he be wearing his cowboy hat tonight?* I wasn't really into cowboys. They weren't really my type, to be honest. But I wasn't exactly going to be picky, either. This cowboy seemed to show interest in me. Good enough. And by no means was he unattractive. He had a very athletic build for his tall frame, his defined muscles showing easily under the slightly too tight T-shirts he always wore. He had a super cute ass in his tight Levi's jeans. Soft brown eyes I could stare at all day. Thick, dark hair that curled just above his ears. Oh. And the dimple on the right side of his cheek that appeared every time he smiled. This was my favourite feature of all. *No. I'm not obsessed in the least bit*, I thought to myself, knowing this to be a complete lie. Just then, Meredith and Molly jumped back into the car, startling me back to reality. Annoyed, I listened to them talk a mile a minute about the two boys in the liquor store they had just met. Apparently, the boys were in the engineering program at the university. And they played on the university volleyball team. Of course. With their height, how could they not?

I was getting impatient. I shivered and looked at the goosebumps that were visible on my arms. It was now 8:17 p.m., and the sun had started to slowly dip, along with the heat of the day.

"Ok, lets get going," I said with a touch of enthusiasm that even surprised me.

Molly and Meredith exchanged a look and a smile, relieved, I'm sure, that I was finally coming to life.

"Why are you in such a rush, Syd?" Molly teased.

I rolled my eyes. "The sooner we get there, the sooner I can get this night over with."

Even as I said this, I had trouble convincing myself of it now. *Maybe I should have a drink or two when I get there.* To calm the nerves that I was feeling as we pulled out of the liquor store parking lot.

We were now on the rural highway heading south to the lake Meredith and I knew so well. We went there almost every weekend in the summer growing up. Our little family of four would head out early, usually on Saturdays, for a full day of swimming or playing in the run-down park, consisting of a rusty swing set, a metal slide that got too hot to go down in the heat of the day, and an old wooden teeter-totter that you were guaranteed to get splinters on—the same park that is still there today. It was a smaller lake with one stretch of beach, the rest surrounded by trees. The beach itself wasn't made up of soft sand by any means. It was mostly made up of little rocks, making it virtually impossible to construct a proper sandcastle. As you looked out at the water, there was one small wooden pier, way off to the left, right next to the trees. It always seemed a bit out of place to me. There really was no reason for it to be situated where it was, off to the side like that, in the shallow water. The reeds sticking out all around it looked like hair blowing on a windy day. I always thought of it as perhaps a mistake. An oddity. But somehow this dock always called to me. I would walk to it when I wanted to get away from the crowd. I would sit at the end of this dock, in the shade of the trees, my only company being that of mosquitos. I guess this was another safe zone of mine, a place I went to when I was overwhelmed by people and noise. I would sit at the end of this dock, kicking my legs back and forth, in deep thought. Until, of course, I was startled back to reality by other kids who had decided to come to my place of escape and horse around. This would always annoy me to no end. Not their problem. They were being normal kids. Perhaps they were annoyed by me.

The sound of the gravel road we were on now brought me back to reality again, along with Meredith turning up the volume to "Crazy Train," a song I enjoyed as well. It was our road trip song, always putting me in a good mood. I found myself tapping my fingers on the steering wheel and singing along to it. As I rounded the corner into the parking lot, it was obvious most people were already here. There were no parking spots left, and I found myself making up a spot on a patch of grass.

I let out a deep sigh as I turned the key and the noise of the music and engine came to an immediate stop. My nerves hit me again, this time with even more intensity. *Holy shit. Ugh.* I started to panic as Meredith and Molly were already out of the car. I could feel an anxiety attack starting to brew in my stomach. Why couldn't I be like Meredith? Why couldn't I just *be* Meredith? I got out of my car slowly, feeling slightly lightheaded. I could see from where I was standing that there was a bonfire on the beach. Members from both teams congregated around the flickering flames, talking and laughing loudly at whatever conversation was being had. Everyone looked so natural in this setting. Meredith and Molly were already across the parking lot, so I started to pick up my feet and move toward them, not wanting to be alone.

I quickly scanned the faces as we approached the crowd and felt immediate relief when Trevor was nowhere to be found. "Thank God," I muttered to myself. *I don't feel ready. Will I ever be ready, though?* I was equally relieved to see Candace and Emily there, two girls I really liked on our team. Not that I disliked any of the other girls, exactly. It's just that I found these two girls to be genuinely friendly and they never spoke in a judgmental or rude way. To put it bluntly, they weren't snobs. They weren't considered to be part of the cool group, because you had to have one of those in any group dynamic, I thought to myself sarcastically. Maybe because they were two of the weaker players on our team? Or maybe because they were just too nice to fit into that category? Not pretty enough? Emily was lanky, her dark hair styled in a short boy cut. Her face showed evidence of her struggles with acne as a teenager. Candace was a short, slightly overweight redhead with not much in the way of soccer skill. But man, could she kick that ball hard and far. Whatever the reason, I gravitated to them the moment I met them. Often, I felt the only reason the other girls even talked to me was because I was one of the more skilled players. Because of this, the other girls were never rude or mean to me. Sadly, this was not always the case for Candace and Emily—another reason I naturally gravitated toward them. I knew what it felt like to be on the outside looking in. I knew it well, so they were easy to relate to. I admired them because any hurtful comments that were directed their way, especially regarding their quality of play, they seemed to just brush off, something I wasn't particularly good at. I took things to heart. My solution was to avoid people in general so I could avoid being hurt in any way. Probably not the best way to go about life.

"Hi, Emily! Hi, Candace! How's it going?" I asked enthusiastically.

"Sydney!" they both yelled in unison.

I was immediately bombarded by both with friendly hugs. This instantly put me at ease as I hugged them back.

"You want a beer?" Candace asked me as she reached into the cooler to pull one out for me.

"No, thanks. I'm driving tonight. Let me know if either of you will need a ride home later."

Just then Molly and Meredith joined us.

"I'll be driving these two drunks home, anyway," I teased, winking at my sister.

Meredith gave me a shot in the arm as she chugged half of her cooler. This resulted in some of the alcohol spilling over and down her chin. We all laughed at this. My sister knew how to have a good time. I'll give her that. And she wasted no time in doing just that. She and Molly danced their way into the crowd and disappeared from my sight.

I decided to take a seat on a log close to the fire. Emily and Candace sat next to me. The beach was now enveloped in darkness except for the flickering flames of the bonfire in front of me. People appeared into the light that the fire provided, then disappeared just as quickly into the fringe of the darkness that surrounded it. I watched the flames dance as the two girls chatted about something I obviously wasn't really interested in. Something about a fight that Candace got into with her mother. Or was it her father? I tuned them out subconsciously as I watched the flames climb higher. The noise of the crowd grew, along with the consumption of alcohol.

I could hear a girl screaming "No, Brayden! Put me down! Seriously... I'm going to murder you if you throw me in! Brayden! No!"

And then the splash of someone getting thrown into the lake, presumably by Brayden. I looked around and watched the girls dancing to the music, trying to get the boys to dance with them. *What a sight*, I thought, as I took it all in. *Just pure abandonment of any possible reservations they may have had before coming here. Gone. Or disguised by the alcohol they all eagerly drank. Maybe I should have that drink*, I thought to myself.

Just then I heard one of the guys call out Trevor's name. Instantly I felt panic as he appeared out of the dark to my right. Just looking at him made me blush as I felt the heat in my body rise, and not from the fire. *God. What's wrong with me? He's just a guy.* I felt that excitement again, not sure what I was expecting from tonight. I was expecting too much, no doubt. I quickly took inventory of him. He was wearing his cowboy hat and a baby blue T-shirt that was of course just slightly too tight on him, tucked neatly into his jeans. He had a leather bracelet on his right wrist and a silver watch on his left. I liked his arms—specifically, his forearms. Not sure why, but I thought they were nice forearms. As my eyes wandered down, I noticed the cowboy boots he had on, thinking this was an odd choice of footwear for a lake party. *What do I know? He had to complete the look, I suppose.* Just as I looked back up, I caught him glancing at me and giving me a smile. That dimple. There it was. I smiled back nervously and quickly turned my attention back to Emily and Candace, pretending to be part of their conversation. I glanced back in his direction again and he was gone. Just like that. Back into the dark. I couldn't help but feel the disappointment that washed over me then. I was hoping that maybe he'd sit beside me at least. I could hear his voice and laughter fade into the background and blend in with everyone else's. Another disappointment. Now I couldn't see him or hear him. *Maybe if I get off this log and mingle, I could possibly run into him again.* Just as I was building up the courage to do just that, Emily and Candace apparently had the same idea, as I peered at the empty spots previously occupied by them. My courage suddenly disappeared. So, I sat there. I sat and watched everyone for nearly an hour, hoping that Trevor would come back and maybe choose to occupy the empty spot next to me. I guess the typical shy, boring wallflower decided to show up tonight. The disappointments just kept coming in waves.

Stargazing

•••

I'm not sure what got me to get up in that moment. Was it the
anger I felt at myself, the annoyance of watching everyone have
a good time, or just the need to stretch my legs out? Whatever
the reason, I knew it had nothing to do with courage. I walked
down the beach to my safe place, to the dock I knew so well. I
pulled my hat down, as if that would make me invisible in some
way, and walked at a brisk pace, trying to distance myself from
the crowd as quickly as possible. I was grateful to notice the
noise of the party fade behind me. My eyes adjusted to the dark
as I looked down the beach, relieved to see the old wooden dock
sitting there, looking as lonely as I felt. As I finally approached it,
in what seemed to take forever, I noticed the wind had picked up.
The trees sounded like they were having an angry conversation
amongst themselves, the leaves and branches their voice as they
rustled in the breeze. I sat down and scanned the lake in front of
me. It was even more shallow on this end than I remembered.
The water must have dropped a bit, I thought to myself. The
reeds and grass around the dock seemed taller than usual. As
I swung my legs back and forth, I noticed just how alone I was.
The black abyss of the water stretched out in front of me, making it seem like I was on a different planet. This planet seemed
to suit me more anyway.

Just then, I heard a voice behind me: "Hey."

The voice was almost whisper quiet, sending my heart to my feet as I nearly jumped out of my skin. I looked back to see a familiar figure stumble toward me, the blue of his shirt almost glowing in the dark. How I didn't notice him approaching is beyond me. The wind could have had a part to play. Not that I was complaining. It was a nice surprise, and it was what I had been waiting for all night, right? A chance to see Trevor again. I just wasn't sure I was ready to be alone with him quite yet.

Stop being such a prude, I told myself.

I didn't even have a chance to recover as he sat to the right of me, oblivious to the fact that I'm sure I looked ghostly, the blood leaving my face slowly from the shock. God, I was such a rookie with this sort of thing... obviously.

I tried to slow my breathing down as I responded with a casual "Hey."

Or at least I thought it sounded casual. I'm sure it was anything but that. It was then that I noticed he didn't have his cowboy hat on. His hair was tussled, giving him a boyish look. The heat I felt radiating off his body made me realize how close he was to me. Suddenly, in that moment, I imagined him putting one gorgeous arm around me and pulling me closer. That's what most girls would want, right? Normal girls my age. I wasn't sure if my heart was speaking to me, or my brain. It seemed like a logical progression. So that is what I imagined.

"What are you doing here by yourself?" he asked. I detected a slur in his words, with the smell of whiskey strong on his breath.

"I don't know. The party was getting a bit boring, I guess. And a bit loud."

He laughed in a way I'm not sure that I appreciated all that much. Scoffing was probably a more accurate description than laughing. It most definitely hit a nerve with me, chipping away a tiny bit of the pedestal I had built beneath him. An aura of dominant arrogance filled the tiny void between whatever space was literally left between us. I suddenly felt on edge. I looked more closely at him and caught the glazed look in his eyes. He was intoxicated. To what degree, I wasn't sure, but it was something I probably shouldn't have been all that surprised with. Literally every single person there was drinking some kind of alcoholic beverage. Everyone but me... so it seemed. I looked past him, back toward the fire. It was just a small flicker of light from this distance. I started to feel a little uneasy now as I realized how far I was from everyone.

"So, you're a twin, hey?" he asked, trying to make awkward small talk.

He obviously knew the answer to this, but I responded anyway.

"Yeah, I'm a twin. Older by five minutes. So what are you doing out here?" I asked, suddenly wondering if he had followed me out. "I mean, why did you come out here? Did you follow me?"

The confusion on his face was almost comical.

"Well yeah, I did. Is there something wrong with that? I just caught a vibe earlier. I smiled at you. You smiled at me. I noticed you come over here. Am I reading this all wrong?"

As I looked at him, I was hoping it was dark enough for him to not see how truly embarrassed I was. I pulled my hat further down to cover as much of my face as I could. *What is wrong with me?!* I was interrogating him, and all he was doing was acting like a normal guy who was interested in a girl. Obviously, I wasn't very subtle with the fact that I liked him as well. After all, he did catch me staring at him on more than one occasion.

"I'm sorry. No, you're not wrong. I guess you just startled me a bit."

Hopefully my apology could salvage any chance I had with him, even if to just continue the conversation. I was surprised he wasn't already walking away. Instead, he smiled at me, his dimple winning me over so easily, again.

"That's ok. All good. Why don't you take your hat off?" he asked, his eyes darting to my safety net. My shield.

So, I did just that. I took my favourite hat off, like the always-so-obedient girl I was. The eternal people pleaser. I didn't want to take my hat off, but I did anyway. I couldn't shake the disappointment in myself, the annoyance I felt at the pit of my stomach. I was like a puppet.

He slid even closer to me, his leg touching mine now, sending shivers through my body. I wasn't sure what I wanted to happen at that point, but I was relieved that he continued the conversation with me, chatting mostly about soccer. This seemed like the natural thing to talk about, the only thing we really knew of each other. We were borderline strangers.

As we chatted, I noticed his hand rest on my thigh, the warmth of his skin feeling nice. At first. It felt like every nerve in my body was alive and on alert. *This is normal.* I kept repeating this over again in my head. *This is normal.* He continued talking, almost as if to distract me from the fact that his hand kept creeping higher up my leg. I wasn't distracted in the least. The words coming out of his mouth ended up being background noise at that point. I started feeling super uncomfortable, but I just sat there, frozen. My brain and my body just froze. I knew that I wasn't ok with what was happening now. So why was I letting him put his hand up my shorts? I continued to stare straight ahead at the black, ominous-looking water while his fingers continued searching, working their way beneath my underwear. With his fingers finally hitting the intended target, I flinched and let out a tiny gasp. Every fibre of my being felt suddenly repulsed. With this, my body and brain came back to life, and I shoved his hand away.

Well, most men, I would assume, would get the hint. Most. Not Trevor. He stared at me briefly, defiantly, squinting at me. Something told me he was not used to rejection. Without warning, he suddenly grabbed the back of my head and pulled me in for a kiss. Except this was no sweet kiss, like the kiss in my dreams. All I could taste was whiskey as he forced his tongue into my mouth. As I tried to pull away, he just tightened his grip on the back of my head and pulled me in even closer, his tongue relentless, searching for some kind of response or reciprocation. I used both of my hands to try to push him away. I don't quite remember if I used my legs as well. It took everything I had to finally separate myself from him.

"What the hell are you doing?" I yelled, breathless and in shock.

Suddenly the features on his face contorted into an angry look. He just glared at me. I wasn't noticing the dimple anymore. "As if you didn't want this! Coming out here, all by yourself. Seriously? You're the ugly twin. Take what you can get." He laughed as he said this last statement.

His words cut through me like the cold wind. I didn't even know how to respond. I just knew I had to get off the dock and back to the fire. I had to find Meredith and Molly. The night I was hoping for was not going to happen. The guy I had dreamed about was not here. I knew that without a doubt. I did not want any part of this version of Trevor. Maybe this was the only version of him. His aggressive behaviour scared me. His aggressive kiss hurt. But his words—"the ugly twin"—somehow hurt so much more. It was like a punch in the gut, something I'd always struggled with internally. Now to hear the words said out loud by someone else... someone who I thought liked me for me... someone who I thought found me attractive enough to show interest in me... *I should have known. I should have listened to my gut. Stupid girl. I should have known...*

I could feel the tears now cascading down my cheeks as I struggled to find my footing to stand up. Of course, Trevor had other ideas and was in no way going to let me just walk away. I had embarrassed him. My rejection angered him. I could see it. I could sense it. The air around me vibrated with his anger. He shoved me back down and I could feel the dock connect with the back of my head. I lay there stunned, the dull pain in my head starting to throb already. I had no time to think or do anything really. He was now on top of me, his jeans and boxers already pulled down to his ankles. He started to fumble with the button on my shorts as I tried to fight him off.

"Get off! Help!" I screamed. Or maybe it was a whisper. Either way, I knew I was on my own. There was no one around to hear my desperate plea. Everyone was by the bonfire that now looked like a flicker from a cigarette lighter from this distance.

This time, my cries for help were stifled instantly as he covered my mouth with one hand.

"Shut up!" he yelled at me angrily.

The look in his eyes terrified me. I don't think I could ever describe accurately what stared back at me in that moment. A wild look. A desperate look. A vacant look. A determined look. The look of a crazed man. A look that made me fear for my life.

It was then that I noticed I couldn't breathe. The weight of him on top of me, his hand covering my mouth. I couldn't breathe as I struggled beneath him. He managed to pull my shorts and underwear down enough to thrust himself inside of me with one quick motion. My body shook from the sobs I was trying to let out. I knew I couldn't fight him. The longer this lasted, the longer I couldn't breathe. This I knew for a fact. I decided to give up the fight in hopes this nightmare would end sooner. So I froze. Again.

It was in this moment that I noticed the stars as I looked past him. Millions of white, sparkling stars on a black canvas. I chose to stare at the beauty of the night sky, a distraction from the ugliness that was happening to me at that moment. As I focused on the stars, suddenly everything went quiet. This possibly could be what an out-of-body experience feels like. It didn't feel like I was in that place anymore. The girl whose innocence was being ripped from her very being was not there. I was numb from it all. I can't tell you exactly how long this lasted. Time stood still. It could have been seconds or minutes. I truly have no idea. I just know when it finally ended, I came crashing back to earth gasping for every ounce of air that I could. He had abruptly stood up and was zipping up his jeans as I struggled to breathe again.

"If you say one fucking word about this, I'll kill you. Better yet, why don't you go and kill yourself? Stupid, ugly whore." He looked nervously around as he spat these last words out. Then he jumped over me and disappeared into the dark.

And just like that, he was gone. I rolled onto my side and started bawling uncontrollably. I curled up, hugging my knees tight to my chest, and just cried. An awful, guttural-sounding cry, like the sound of a wounded animal. That cry that comes from deep within your soul. As I tried wiping the tears off my face, I caught a glimpse of my hat on the dock beside me and grabbed it, like it was going to fix everything. I put it back on my head instinctively. Habit, I guess. There was no one to hide from out here in the dark by myself. But it was my magical hat, and there was nothing more that I wanted to do just then but to disappear.

The Recruit

My legs started to shake as I struggled to keep my form. As the constable stood over me, the sweat on my chin started to drip onto my forearms. The first day of recruit training was a scorcher, the sun beating down on my back already at 9:00 a.m.

"Hansen! You call that a plank? Flatten that back!"

The fact that I was even hired into policing was a feat, considering my age: forty-six years old. I was only one of five females in a class of thirty-two recruits. I'd like to think it was my personality that got me this gig. My love of meeting people, talking to absolutely anyone and everyone, my passion to help people, to have a meaningful career, were all factors contributing to this driving force to go after it. It's something I've always wanted to do since I can remember. My family and friends, of course, had their opinions, which I mostly just ignored. Nothing was going to stop me from at least trying. No one's opinion, comments, judgmental remarks... nothing. I was a stubborn fool, maybe. But at least I wouldn't be left wondering if I could have made it. I had the answer for myself now.

"Get up there! Go, go, go!"

I couldn't tell if the constable's face was red from anger or the heat. Regardless, I jumped up to my feet with the rest of my class and started running up the wooden stairs that zigzagged up the steep hill. The railing was lined with constables, sergeants, staff sergeants, and a couple of inspectors who stood out in their white uniforms. As we passed each one, we had to address them formally. If we got their rank wrong, we were yelled at. If we were too slow, we were yelled at. If we stumbled, we were yelled at. If our breathing was too loud, we were yelled at. If we looked at them the wrong way, we were yelled at. It was an hour of the recruit staff screaming at us for absolutely everything we did or didn't do. It was quite comical, not bothering me in the least. Maybe my age had something to do with it, seeing that I was probably older than at least half of the training staff and the oldest in the entire recruit class. The looks on the faces of my classmates told me that this was not something they knew how to handle. I could clearly see by their wide-eyed expressions that they were scared. I felt like telling them that it was ok. The training staff were just normal human beings, and what they were showing us was not their real personalities. I knew enough to know it was a show, a game to push us mentally.

I ran past Thom and Sparks and another recruit who was puking off to the side. At my age, I was in decent shape. And my youthful appearance probably didn't give away my age to my classmates. A blessing, for now. I got to the top and saw Staff Sergeant Dickson. He broke into a big smile and offered me words of encouragement.

"Keep it up, Hansen!"

I smiled back, turned around, and ran back down the stairs, a burst of energy and motivation now carrying me through. It was Staff Sergeant Dickson who took the chance on me and hired me. "Recruit Constable Hansen"... it had a nice ring to it, I thought to myself.

We continued the training session for an hour in the heat, with no break. It was grueling, exhausting, and fun at the same time. I encouraged my classmates throughout the session, trying to ignore my burning lungs and the heavy feeling in my legs. I was not about to show any weakness this early on in training. And I was not going to disappoint Staff Sergeant Dickson.

As we were finishing up, I could hear an ambulance in the distance. We were in a circle formation now, sitting on the grass, the stretching being led by Recruit Constable Bennett. I reached for my toes, feeling the tightness of my hamstrings. The sound of the siren became increasingly louder. They were coming for Recruit Constable Norton, who I saw puking earlier in the workout. He was hunched over with his head between his legs. A couple of the training members were kneeling beside him. *Poor guy*, I thought to myself. Not a great impression on only the first day. But could you blame him?

As I walked to the parking lot, toward my car, I noticed six of my classmates standing and conversing with one another. Perfect; this was my opportunity to meet some of them.

I strolled over to the group, doing a quick scan. There were two women and four men. Two of the men were at least six feet tall, lanky, and both had short buzz cuts. They looked like they could almost be brothers. One had blond hair, the other dark brown. Both Caucasian. One of the other males was quite short, broad in stature, with darker skin and dark black hair. The fourth male was of average height, Caucasian as well, with a muscular, athletic build. I distinctly remember him as one of the more fit individuals in our training session. He was also the one who led the stretch at the end, Recruit Constable Bennett. He was probably half my age, but I found him to be very attractive. My guess is he would be one of the more popular recruits in our class, and most definitely a favourite of the trainers. The two women in the group were a stark contrast from one another. The one girl was quite tall. She had beautiful red hair pulled tight into a neat bun, gorgeous pale skin, and a muscular build. She looked to be in her early twenties. The other woman I had trouble envisioning passing the minimal physical requirements to even get hired. But she kept up, and as life has taught me, looks can be deceiving. It was tough to guess her age just by looking at her. She was also Caucasian, short in stature, with mousy brown hair and kind brown eyes. She may not have been the most fit female there, but I couldn't deny how perfect her hair bun was. Even after the strenuous workout, not a hair was out of place. I can only imagine the amount of hair spray she must have used. My bun was a disaster from the get-go. It had taken me a half an hour that morning to just put up a half-decent-looking bun.

I approached the group now and said hello.

"Hey, Hansen. Great work out there."

"Thanks, Bennett. You as well."

Our last names were printed on the backs of our shirts, thankfully. There was no way I'd remember thirty-one names. We made small talk for about ten minutes, mostly talking about the weather and what to expect. There would be plenty of time to get to know everyone, though. We said our goodbyes and I hoisted myself into my black GMC Denali, cranking the air conditioner to full blast. As I sat there, feeling the cool air on my face, I couldn't help but smile. *Day one complete. I did it.* I still had trouble believing I was there. I knew there was so much more work to do in training. But I let myself enjoy that moment. This was just the beginning.

Blessed

I pulled into the driveway and walked into the modest bungalow I share with my husband and two teenage sons. I live across the street from a golf course, in a quiet neighbourhood, lined with mature trees. It is one of the older neighbourhoods. In fact, I thought to myself, the first neighbourhood built in the area. Every house on the block was different, each one with its own unique curb appeal. That's what I love about living here. The newer areas hardly had any trees, and every house looked the same, none of them standing out on their own.

"Ethan! Jesse!" I yelled, wondering if either of my boys were home, as I threw my car keys on the counter. Jesse came out of his room just then.

"How was training today, Mom? Did you do anything cool?"

"Nothing cool yet," I said with a laugh.

I knew what he wanted to know. If I had started firearms training. Or tactics. Or driving. Unfortunately, it was only the first day, which consisted of a lot of running, and a lot of yelling. I was excited to try all the things I knew Jesse was inquiring about. In time I would.

"Hey, Mom." Ethan had just come from the basement.

"How was school?" I asked.

"Good," they both responded.

Ethan went out the back door to jump on the trampoline. Jesse went to the living room to play his video games. Both of my boys were good boys. I felt blessed just then. Raising them seemed effortless. They never gave me any problems.

The boys have different personalities—something I am grateful for. Ethan is the jock. He is passionate about hockey but loves doing anything active. Anything he tries, he is good at. He is a natural gifted athlete. No fear in the kid. None. Confidence has never been an issue for him. He has a sense of humour I'd like to say came from me. But my husband, Brett, would of course disagree. Jesse, on the other hand, is the quiet introvert. He tried hockey for a few years but had decided to quit last season. I was happy he had the courage to tell us he didn't enjoy it anymore. The last thing I would want was to have either of them do something they didn't enjoy. I missed watching him play, but I could see how much happier he was. Jesse is the conversationalist. I can talk to him about anything and everything. He is the inquisitive type. Always checking in with me. Always asking how I am doing. Not that Ethan didn't care. It just isn't his personality. But I know both my boys care for me and love me. They just have different ways of showing it. I'd like to assume they are proud of their mother, going after my dream and accomplishing my goal. I wanted to show them that you can do anything you want in life. Literally anything, at any age, with the right mindset.

Just then, Brett walked in the back door, a smile on his face when he saw me standing in the kitchen.

"Well?! How was today?"

"I survived."

He looked relieved and came to give me a hug. He was covered in dust, the result of working in construction. I pushed him away playfully and told him I was going to take a quick shower.

Brett. With his wavy, brown hair and slightly red beard. I love his beard. I mostly love the way it tickles my lips when we kiss. He has the softest brown eyes that just reflect kindness. He is the most empathetic, affectionate, caring man I have ever known. Rarely shows anger. His calm demeanour is something to be admired. He hardly ever comes home in a bad mood. I make up for the both of us in that department.

And he is mine. I know how lucky I am. *Have I ever told him this?* I thought to myself. Probably not. I wasn't the type of person to show affection or talk about feelings and things. Brett, on the other hand, is not afraid to show his affection for me. Something I've tried to stifle over the years, as I am easily embarrassed by it in a public setting. It brings out my shy side. I knew it was something I needed to work on. But it was a hard thing to change after being that way for so many years. I couldn't help but think of that young girl—the one in the coffee shop. The shy, awkward girl who couldn't even make eye contact. I wasn't sure why I was just thinking of her now. I shook away the thought of her and grabbed a towel from the linen closet.

Although the day was officially over at the campus, I still had things to do. I hopped in the shower, then crawled into my cozy flannel pajamas in record time, feeling exhausted. I so badly wanted to go to bed just then, but instead I pulled my parade boots out and started to polish them. I put my music on and polished away. It was surprisingly relaxing. Brett took care of supper, without complaint. He is my angel. Truly. I knew I was absolutely blessed to have this man in my life, supporting me on this unexpected journey at this stage in our lives. Knowing we would all be sacrificing things to see my dream come to reality. I love him more now than the day he asked me to marry him.

Bloodied and Bruised

I tried to stop the blood from dripping out of my nose onto the blue mat. But it was futile. The red spots stood out like splattered paint on a blue canvas. Just then my stomach churned, and I started dry heaving... ready to puke at any moment from the taste of my own blood. That gross, metallic taste... One of my classmates came with a bucket just in time. I started spitting the blood into the bucket as I was on my hands and knees, trying desperately not to fall over.

"I'm so sorry!"

Recruit Constable Walton knelt beside me with a distraught look on his face.

We had just been working in partners; one person was the officer, the other the subject. The idea was for the officer to grab the subject behind the head and swing them to one side to get them off balance, then essentially knee them in the face at the end of the maneuver. The subject was supposed to be holding a mat in front of their face to avoid direct contact from the officer's knee. Constable Lieu decided on this day to partner the smallest person in the class, myself, with one of the tallest. Walton was not used to my size. I was about thirty pounds lighter than the next female. In his defense, I don't think he realized how easy it would be to do this maneuver on me. He swung me much harder than he intended to. As a result, my feet left the ground. The mat, which was supposed to be protecting my face from his knee, was instead used to prevent myself going face-first into the ground. Big mistake. My face, left unprotected, met the full force of Walton's knee. And here I was now, trying desperately to not throw up.

"It's ok, Matt. I'll be fine," I reassured him.

He did not look convinced, and I certainly did not feel convinced myself.

It was only 11:15 a.m.; the day was just getting started. Except my day ended right then and there. The class was told to take a break, with Recruit Constable Walton reluctantly leaving my side. I couldn't help but notice the annoyed look on Lieu's face. Zero empathy in his expression. Like I asked to be kneed in the face.

I was helped up by a couple of my classmates and led to the nurse's office. I don't recall who exactly helped. I don't remember much except for lying on the bed and staring at the white ceiling tiles, trying to focus on something so the room would stop spinning. I do recall that Constable Little had come in at some point and was speaking softly with the nurse.

Constable Little had a boyish look to him and a kind soul. He often pulled me aside to offer me words of encouragement whenever I doubted myself. Which was often these days. He was one of a few who did this if I was noticeably struggling. The other trainers would try and intimidate us to get a better performance. I understood that it was a role they had to play. I did not respond well to it, though. It was not my learning style. I excelled with encouragement, not fearing failure, then getting screamed at when I did fail. Others responded well to that pressure. Not me.

It was 2:40 p.m. when I woke up to the nurse typing away on her computer. I tried focusing on her fingers. They moved so quickly and effortlessly across the keyboard. It was very impressive. She was a petite Asian lady with flawless, porcelain skin. She was beautiful. Just then she turned to look at me with a warm, kind smile. I hadn't noticed until then that I was crying, soft tears falling down my cheeks as I looked at her.

"How are you feeling?"

It took me a moment to register that the question was directed at me. I really was feeling groggy. So this must be what a concussion felt like. I had no doubt I suffered one.

"Not great," I responded.

I'm not sure why, but I started crying uncontrollably then. I couldn't even stop the tears if I wanted to. And I didn't care at this point. She reached over her desk and passed me a tissue. I grabbed it thankfully and tried to dab the tears away. Something about this woman gave me an immense feeling of comfort. It had been three hard months of being scrutinized by the instructors, constantly. This small room, with this friendly, kind face staring back at me... the relief I felt was enormous. I was so thankful for this beautiful woman at that moment.

"You don't belong here. This is not what you were meant to do."

She said this without hesitation, but with a tender voice, as if to soften the blow of the message she was trying to convey to me. But the comment landed bluntly. It hit me hard. Not because I necessarily disagreed with her, but because she was confirming the seed of doubt that was already planted in my mind.

I was struggling to keep up with the rest of my class. This was no secret. I struggled in most areas. I could blame this on possibly a few factors...

I didn't learn or pick up on things as quickly as my classmates. Most were baby adults, fresh out of school. Learning new things was second nature to them. The grey matter in my brain was aging as we speak. But I knew age was a poor excuse. I knew this to be true. I was already proof of that. I was here... at forty-six years old. I learned things at a slower rate, but I was still learning the material. It just took me a bit longer. No... age wasn't the real issue. Being afraid to make mistakes was.

I was a perfectionist. No one was harder on me than myself. The more I struggled, the more I would take it to heart. I took mistakes harder than most. Every mistake crushed me. My classmates would make mistakes, brush it off, and continue with their day. Not me. The negative self-talk would take over. The confidence I had at the start of class was nowhere to be found now. *What is it called again? Imposter syndrome?*

Another factor to consider: I had no doubt that my very small stature was the reason the tactical instructors had been tougher on me then the rest of my class. Their job was to make sure we were properly trained for the streets. With this type of work, size can matter in certain situations. So, as a result, I had to be that much more aggressive, that much more authoritative when I spoke, the volume of my voice that much louder, that much more everything. This higher standard that they were expecting me to meet felt unattainable. I failed miserably.

Which brings me to my last issue... I don't have an aggressive bone in my body. None. Zero. This entire time, they'd been trying to bring out a side of me I knew did not exist. They'd been trying to turn on some switch in me. The funny thing is, there is no switch. At least not the one they were looking for. I am who I am. This was why I dreaded tactical days. I would freeze most of the time, while a classmate would pin me down, or put me in a hold I was expected to get out of. I got used to tuning out the yelling by the instructors.

"Why do you think this isn't meant for me?" I asked her, as I continued to dab away the tears.

I needed to hear someone else tell me what I didn't want to face. My family and friends kept encouraging me to keep going. To keep battling. Of course they would. But here was the class occupational health nurse, who I had met once on our second day of training. Someone I hadn't said more than two words to until that day. An outsider who I knew would be objective. I wanted to hear her reasoning. I needed to hear it. I needed to hear another voice besides the voice in my head.

"The first time I saw you, I knew. You exude kindness and empathy. I see the kindness in your eyes. In your smile. You've been fighting yourself, because deep down you don't want to change. This job will change you."

I cringed at these words. And I was hoping she would stop there. No such luck.

"This job will harden you. It's the nature of the work. Why would you want to change? You have life experience to know better. The others are younger, easier to mold. Maybe a bit naïve. Maybe a bit like robots. The qualities you have are meant to be used through a different channel. Not this one. Your strengths aren't meant to be used here. This is not your path. This job attracts a certain kind of person. You are not that type of person."

Ouch. Her words were like little daggers, with every word slowly torturing me. Did she stop? Nope. The torturing wasn't quite over yet.

"And you couldn't hurt a mouse if you tried. I'm sorry if this sounds harsh... but after years of being the nurse here, I just know."

Nailed it! Just like that. It was truth she spoke. And I knew it.

I sat with this for a few minutes. I rolled over and stared back up at the ceiling. The tears started to spill over again. A part of me was angry, but a sense of relief washed over the other part of me. Maybe she was right? *I'm fighting myself. I've been fighting myself the entire time.*

All the hard work, all the blood, sweat, and tears, to come to this point... I knew I had a choice. To keep going down this path that I always thought was destined for me... or to jump off this road and follow a new, uncertain path.

Drumroll, please...

I chose the first path. Did I ever tell you how stubborn I am? The one factor that trumps all the previous ones that I've mentioned. Age, size, fear of making mistakes, lack of aggression... they had nothing on my stubbornness. This I knew of myself.

Also, the thought of the judgment that would come if I quit was enough to keep me going. Probably not a great reason to keep going. But it was a reason, nonetheless.

Bang! Bang! I'm Dead...

As I drove down the freeway, the sprawling police campus slowly disappeared out of my view as I passed it. I quickly put my sunglasses on. Yes, it was a beautiful, sunny day, but that was not the purpose of putting them on. I needed to hide my tear-streaked face. The traffic was at a standstill now, and I didn't have the luxury of tinted windows to hide behind. The drive home took what seemed like forever. All I wanted to do was get home, put on my pajamas, and crawl into bed.

Finally, I pulled onto my long, uneven, and cracked driveway, shut the car off, and took a deep breath. My family was not going to see my tears of defeat today. *What kind of role model am I for my boys? Not a very good one.* I waved at my neighbour who was walking her two dogs past the house. Gave her a fake, happy smile and waited for her to disappear around the corner. Then I got out.

From the trunk I pulled my son Jesse's old hockey bag, which I had repurposed for carrying all my tactical gear for class, and lugged it into the house. Dropping it awkwardly onto the floor was how I announced my presence every day. Except at this moment, there was thankfully no one to announce it to. Ethan was at hockey practice. Jesse was at a friend's house. And Brett was still at work. So, I robotically walked to my bedroom and did what I had been waiting to do all day. I put my pajamas on and crawled into bed.

Slowly my family came home one by one, my boys asking me how my day was. Of course, I said it went well. I was just tired. Then Brett came home. He walked into the bedroom, and he knew otherwise.

"Not a good day?"

I nodded my head... yes, another horrible day.

Brett came and sat beside me and asked me if I wanted to talk about it. Of course I didn't. I'm sure he was tired of hearing my struggles. He had suggested I quit more than once already, stating that this was not worth my mental health.

"I'm dead, Brett. Right now, if I were working on the street as a police officer... I would have been shot dead. We did scenarios today. I walked into a scene with my partner that was a call for a welfare check. The subject grabbed a gun that was lying on his bed. Pointed it at me. You know what I did? I went for my baton first. My baton! By the time I switched to grab my gun, he had shot me multiple times. I'd be dead. You would have a dead wife. My boys would have a dead mother!"

With this last statement, Brett crawled into the bed with me and just hugged me. The Brett hug I adore. He let me cry it out. It wasn't until I turned around to face him that I noticed he had been crying, too.

Roosevelt

Just another typical day for me, I thought sarcastically to myself. I found myself trying to fight back the tears as I followed the tactical instructors into an empty classroom. Too many tears they'd witnessed from me up to that point. So, I was trying hard to fight these ones back. I felt like I was unravelling at the seams. Climbing up the sloped floor, I finally threw myself into one of the chairs and pulled my hat down, hoping that would make me invisible. No hiding here.

"Hansen. What's going on? We can't help you if you don't tell us what's going on inside that head of yours."

I looked to my right at a concerned Constable Buchanan, one of the only tactical instructors I liked. He was hunched on his heels in the aisle next to my chair, looking at me, waiting for an answer that I didn't really have. I truly didn't know what was wrong. I had just failed tactical scenarios again. While the rest of my fellow recruits headed to our fitness class, I was pulled out and told I'd instead be doing more of these scenarios. And I kept failing them. Miserably.

"Do you mind taking your hat off? So I can see you."

Now I turned to my left, where Staff Sergeant Dalton had seated himself uncomfortably close to me. Two seats over, to be exact. I only say *uncomfortable* because he literally was the most intimidating man I'd ever met on our first day of tactical training.

As lead of the tactical team, I guess you needed to be that way. However, when I looked closely at him this time, I didn't feel any of this intimidation. His eyes looked kind, concerned. The same look that Constable Buchanan gave me. You can really tell a lot about a person by looking at their eyes.

I reluctantly took my hat off, as he had asked. I'm pretty sure what he saw in my eyes was the look of defeat and despair.

Staff Sergeant Dalton continued speaking to me.

"Can I tell you a quote? It's from Eleanor Roosevelt."

"Sure," I replied in a flat tone.

He proceeded with, "No one can make you feel inferior without your consent."

We sat there for a moment while I processed these words. *Strong words*, I thought to myself. I was so grateful in that moment for this kindness he showed me. Essentially, don't let someone's words have power over you. Don't let someone's words or actions make you feel less than. You have a choice: to absorb it or deflect it. *Great. Awesome. A little too late now.* I didn't even recognize the person sitting in this chair anymore. The confident person who had shown up to training was long gone. Now the tears started to come. They'd seen these tears before. No use trying to pretend I was anything but this broken human. *I can't fool them now. Or myself. Why didn't I listen to the nurse six weeks ago? Why am I still here?*

The Message

I felt bad leaving Meredith and Molly at the party last night, but I knew they'd find a way home. It wasn't a decision the usually responsible Sydney would make. But I felt like I deserved a pass on this one. So, I ditched my sister and friend. Without hesitation. There was no way I was going to tell them what happened. I decided right then that no one would ever know. It was a secret I was going to take to my grave.

I rolled out of bed and made my way to the bathroom. Probably should have stayed in bed. My eyes were so swollen that my pupils could hardly be seen through the now small opening between my eyelids. I cried so many tears that there was nothing left to cry. My hand gently stroked the small goose egg on the back of my head. I noticed a dull pain and a burning sensation as I squinted down to inspect what else was damaged. *Damaged... a suitable word*, I thought to myself. I let my pajama pants fall to the floor. There was small blotchy bruising between my thighs, but what stood out more was how red my skin was. I knew this was from scrubbing my skin raw in the shower last night. A shower that couldn't cleanse me, no matter how long I let the scalding-hot water wash over me. It didn't matter how hard I scrubbed... I felt dirty; I felt disgusting. The words he said to me... etched in my brain like carved letters in concrete. I knew it would be hard to erase this night from my memory. But I was going to have to try. I had to. Because at that very moment I wanted to die. I wanted to join my now-dead plant and just be done with it. Be done with everything. Forget or die.

Well, I guess I was wrong... I had plenty of tears left to cry. I crawled back into bed and stayed there for a week, telling my boss that I had the bad case of the stomach flu. Telling my family the same thing. Avoiding Dorothy's constant knocking on my door. Avoiding any contact with the outside world as I cried and cried. An endless flow of tears. And thoughts of dying. Just like Trevor suggested. Maybe life was trying to tell me this all along? But I wasn't listening. Until a messenger in the form of a monster delivered it to me. A monster disguised as a handsome cowboy. With that dimple added for good measure. *Stupid, ugly girl...*

Easy-Peasy...

...

I sat on a bed in a small, cold room, waiting for the doctor to see me. I went over what I would say as I stared at the cracks in the black leather. For a month I had somehow managed to keep my thoughts of ending my life from turning into reality. Maybe to spare my family. But mostly because deep down I knew I could never actually go through with it. I was a coward at heart. But the thoughts were always there. *Would anyone really miss me? How would I do it? When would I do it? Where would I do it?* Sprinkle in the constant breakdowns I had in private... well, the mere task of getting out of bed every day was a feat. It was a struggle to put on my everyday mask, the mask everyone expected of me, then ripping it off to breathe when no one was looking. I just wanted it to stop. I wanted this roller coaster to stop. I didn't want to feel anymore. I didn't want to feel sad or angry, or even happy. I just didn't want to feel. Period.

Just then, an older gentleman walked into the room, startling me. I had seen this doctor once before. He was thin and short in stature, only his white beard giving away that he was, in fact, an older gentleman. Someone who wouldn't really startle anyone. But lately, everything made me a bit jumpy.

"So, what can I do for you, young lady?"

He didn't bother to look up at me as he asked this question. Instead, he continued to stare at his clipboard, I assume to read up on my history or whatever. I didn't respond right away. That's when he finally looked up. Sometimes silence can speak a thousand words.

"I just feel sad all the time. I don't know why." I said this quickly. And bluntly. No sense beating around the bush. I wanted to get in and out as fast as humanly possible.

Of course, I knew why. But I was not about to go telling a stranger the details of my why. I just wanted to be prescribed something, anything that would help numb me.

"Anything out of the ordinary happen? Anything outside of your regular routine? A trauma? Or a death in the family?"

He asked me these questions casually. Like if I had loose stool with my nausea. Or a cough with my cold. No biggie. To him. I could tell he had been doing this for too long. Not an ounce of empathy or concern was detected in his voice. His eyes looked bored. He just saw me as another patient asking to be medicated. Good. It was just what I wanted and expected. It was the precise reason I picked this older male doctor again. It was the same vibe I had felt when I had gone in for a pap smear not too long ago.

Mission accomplished. Boom. "Here you go." I was amazed at how easily they prescribed medications. I walked out of the medi-clinic with a prescription in my hand for Prozac, an antidepressant. I think it was safe to say I met the criteria. It was the first time I felt hopeful. A sense of relief washed over me as I climbed into my car. *Please, please work. Numb me, God damn it. Just numb me from the world.*

Last Straw

Another gruelling day of training. For me, anyway. The rest of the recruits were in fitness class again. Not me. Here I was again in the mat room. Pulled out of class to do more scenarios. Except these scenarios were much harder than any of the earlier ones I was made to do.

"Drop the screwdriver! Drop it now!"

I screamed at Constable Powell, who was playing the role of a subject trying to break into a house.

The 'subject' let the screwdriver drop out of his left hand and fall to the floor. He then turned and started to walk toward me in an aggressive manner. I started to back up and yelled for him to stay where he was. Now let me paint you a picture of Constable Powell. He was at least six feet five in height, if not taller. And he was thick. A beast of a man. I decided to pull my baton out and whack him in the legs when he finally reached me.

"Get back!" I screamed.

Whack! Whack! Whack! Nothing. He just kept coming toward me. I stumbled and fell on my back. *God, I suck.*

"Ok, stop!"

Constable Burton killed the scenario. A mercy kill. *Thank the lord.* I struggled to my feet and stood there as three of the constables circled me like sharks. Constable Powell, Constable Burton, and Constable Dick, all waiting to take a bite out of me.

This was the part they seemed to enjoy. Whether they did, I have no idea. Constable Lieu, however, remained seated in a corner of the mat room, sipping his coffee and looking as smug as ever. Like he knew I would fail. Like he wanted me to fail. The only friendly face was that of Constable Little, who was only there to videotape the scenarios.

"Do you think Constable Powell could have killed you with his bare hands?" Constable Burton asked me with a calm voice. He was always calm, a feature I did appreciate with him.

"Of course he could have. And probably would have," I replied, my voice starting to tremble.

"Then why didn't you pull your gun out?" Burton asked. I could hear the frustration in his voice.

I replied, equally frustrated, "Because I had a strip torn off me a few weeks ago when Constable Striden came at me with just his bare hands. I pulled my gun out then, because I'm pretty sure all 240 pounds of him could still kill me with those bare hands."

"That was a different circumstance," Constable Burton replied.

"It was the exact same circumstance! Both coming at me with no weapon in their hands!"

Of course, I knew I was wrong. Both scenarios were different in circumstance. I knew this. It was a desperate answer. I was feeling desperate.

I surprised myself with how angry my response was. They were surprised, as well. I stood in that mat room for almost an hour and a half while they grilled me, trying to defend my choices as best as I could. Futile. Absolutely useless. I finally came to the realization that it didn't matter what choice I made or what answer I gave them. They were done with me. They wanted me out. I wasn't the right fit for the job. And I couldn't have agreed with them more. They did their job. They succeeded in weeding me out. I couldn't even fault them for that. So, I made it easy for them.

It was when some spit flew out of Constable Dick's mouth, in the middle of his angry rant, and landed in my right eye, that I finally snapped.

I wiped my eye in a slow, deliberate motion, the anger in me finally reaching its boiling point.

I stared at Constable Dick and yelled, "Back off! I quit!"

As I started walking toward the door, Constable Little chased after me, pleading with me not to quit.

"Don't quit, Hansen! Don't say those words!"

I adored this man. My in-house therapist. But even his words could not change my mind. I wasn't meant to be there. I knew that now without a doubt. This wasn't meant for me. Why did I have to be so goddamn stubborn?

Sleepover

...

A few weeks had passed since I started my new medication. I was starting to feel human again. Just last weekend I managed to play some crib with Dorothy. My first real outing. She managed to stay sober, so I lost every game we played. Her real motivation for staying sober was obvious, though. She was worried. She was terrible at acting casual when she was worried about me. She didn't hide it very well. She sucked at it. She oozed concern. A million questions. How I was? How was the party? Was I ok? Did anything happen? Was I telling her everything? I dodged every question effortlessly. I had my mask on, and with this new medication, it was easier to keep this mask on. So, I played it cool. Like everything was hunky-dory. At least I think I had her convinced. I was impressed with my acting abilities. Much better than hers.

Tonight, Meredith and I were planning to go to Molly's for a sleepover. Watch movies. Eat popcorn. I could manage that, I thought. No sweat. I was slowly starting to appear back into the land of the living.

Molly lived on an acreage with her parents on the outskirts of town. Meredith picked me up at around 8 p.m. I decided on the most comfortable clothing possible. My flannel pajamas. Why not? It was a sleepover, right?

As I jumped into her car she asked, "How's it going, sis?"

"Good! Everything is good!" I replied in the most positive tone I could possibly muster. I really was getting good at this.

With that, she smiled, and we were off. I did detect a sense of relief in her smile. But could I blame her? I literally shut myself off from the world. I just went to work. Then I went home. I mean, it really wasn't too different from my regular routine. I had yet to see my parents, though. I'd have to make a point to visit them soon.

Most of the car ride, we sat in silence. I stared out the window at the rows of houses that soon turned into rows of trees as we got further out of town. Their leaves were starting to turn golden as fall was approaching. This was usually my favourite time of year. I closed my eyes, pretending to sleep, only to avoid conversation with Meredith. We finally pulled onto a gravel driveway and parked in front of a modest-sized house sitting on top of a hill. I could see a beautiful pond at the bottom of the hill out back. The property was surrounded by trees. This place was beautiful. Peaceful. I loved everything about it. A contrast to my lonely and empty apartment that was the place of nightmares now. Countless times I'd woken up in my bed, screaming and punching the air in front of me. It usually ended up with me falling out of bed with my duvet wrapped around me. Every night, this battle with literally no one woke me up.

Just then Molly came running out the door to greet us.

"Hey guys! Come in!"

Before we walked into the house, I asked, "Where are all your farm animals? I don't see any animals."

"Oh. My. God," Molly responded in disbelief. "Are you serious?! We live on an acreage. Not a farm. There's a difference!"

"Oh... sorry. I'm a city slicker," I responded with embarrassment.

"No shit," Molly replied, rolling her eyes.

I laughed at this. And I mean, I really laughed. I almost-peed-my-pants laughed. We all laughed. And it felt great. Even if I did sound uneducated, I didn't care.

We walked into a very large, bright kitchen. Larger than what I was used to. The walls were lined with endless oak cabinets. I'd never seen so many cabinets. *What on earth do they fill them with?!* Immediately to my left were stairs that went down to the basement. We walked through the kitchen to an even larger living room. It had a vaulted ceiling with a wood beam that went across the entire length. This was the definition of cozy. Everything about this place seemed cozy. I could even hear the deafening sound of the frogs down by the pond. It felt like I was at a retreat at some cabin. I was in love with this place.

"Where are your parents?" Meredith asked curiously.

"They're at the neighbours' down the road," Molly replied as she pulled out some nachos and began shredding some cheddar cheese.

We finally settled onto the couch in the living room and watched *Pretty Woman*. Apparently, this was Molly's favourite movie of all time. She didn't mind watching it again for the millionth time. We pigged out on popcorn and a plate of nachos and cheese. The bloating didn't bother me in the least. It felt good to veg out with company for once.

Just then the door to the front of the house came crashing open. All I could hear were a couple of male voices. The voices faded as they went down to the basement.

"Don't mind my older brother and his friend. I'm sure they're drunk," Molly said with a tinge of annoyance in her voice.

Drunk males. Not my favourite, I thought to myself. I flashed back to that night, my eyes starting to well up with tears. Quickly, I got up to use the bathroom. *Pull yourself together*, I scolded myself as I dabbed the tears away, staring at myself in the mirror. I quickly tossed the tissue into the garbage can and walked out.

I was grateful Molly and Meredith were more interested in watching what was on the screen, not noticing my abrupt exit. We watched one more movie before we decided to go to bed. Molly's parents' bedroom was upstairs. The rest of the bedrooms were downstairs, so that's where we headed. As we approached the first bedroom downstairs, on the left, Molly swung open the door and walked in.

I could hear her ask "Were you using this?"

Without waiting for a response, she walked out with a pillow.

"Yes, I was using it."

I could only assume it was the voice of her annoyed brother. She was obviously short one pillow, I thought to myself, amused. Even with his sister pulling his own pillow from underneath his head as he tried to fall asleep, there was still no anger in his voice. Slight annoyance, but that was it. I detected a calmness in that voice. A kind voice.

Meredith and I followed Molly to her bedroom. It was a surprisingly small bedroom, with just enough room for her queen-size bed and a dresser. We crammed into her bed and chattered on for what seemed like hours, talking about anything and everything. Just what the doctor ordered. A distraction for my brain. I felt my eyes getting heavy, only hearing every other word now. It was the first time I closed my eyes and had a peaceful sleep in what seemed like forever.

The next morning, I woke up to an empty bed. I could hear Meredith and Molly upstairs making way too much noise. They were making breakfast. I could smell the bacon. I decided to lounge in bed for a while longer, enjoying the extra room I had now.

As I pulled the duvet up to my chin, I heard the same male voices again upstairs, assuming they were that of her brother and his friend. I couldn't quite make out what they were saying. Suddenly I felt nervous. I don't know why. I felt nervous to go upstairs knowing they were there. *Stop it*, I thought to myself. Then I remembered that all I wore to Molly's house were my flannel pajamas. The thought of walking up the stairs and having them see me wearing pj's horrified me. *Ugh.*

I rolled myself out of the bed and went to the basement bathroom to brush my teeth. *At least I'll have fresh-smelling breath.*

I couldn't drag this out all day, so I finally made my way up the stairs to the kitchen. Of course both boys were sitting at the table, both turning to look at me. *Would it look ridiculous if I ran back down the stairs?* It was too late, I thought to myself. They saw my entirety. Flannel pajamas and all. I just stood there, feeling my face get flushed and hot with embarrassment.

I did a quick scan of both in the small amount of time I was afforded before I was expected to speak. Both handsome. Of course. Couldn't catch a break. The first guy I glanced at was stocky, with an athletic build and beautiful blue eyes, his straight, brown hair tousled from sleep. The other one was taller, with a lean build. He had curly, brown, shoulder-length hair. But it was his eyes that grabbed my attention. Soft, gentle, golden-brown eyes.

He was the first to stand up and offer me his hand. "Hi. My name is Brett."

There was that kind voice I recognized from the night before...

The Couch

I was a disaster since I made the difficult decision to quit my police training. This was my fourth visit now to see Katherine. Although I fought the idea of going to therapy, I knew I wasn't ok. I knew I needed help. I didn't have it in me to pretend everything was fine. Brett and the boys knew me well enough to know if I was faking it. So, there was no point in putting in the effort. Instead, they saw the broken version. The version who felt like an absolute failure and disappointment to everyone.

So here I was, sitting on her oversized couch again, hoping she could put me back together. I couldn't help but notice that my right leg was shaking as I tried to avoid her gaze. I always tried to avoid making eye contact with her. But it was a small room.

I looked up as she continued to speak, trying to focus on her words.

"So, we've talked a bit about your family background and up-bringing, and your recent police experience. You've also alluded to this past 'trauma' a few times in our conversations. A trauma you haven't told anyone about. We've kind of danced around the topic. Are you comfortable putting a name to it yet?"

I just stared at her for a moment. Then I stared at the tattoo on the inside of my right forearm. The Eleanor Roosevelt quote

I was told a few months ago... now permanently etched into my skin. As a reminder.

"Yes," I responded in a robotic tone.

I knew I couldn't avoid it forever. And these sessions weren't cheap. So, I tried to do exactly that. To put a name to it, like she suggested. But the silence that followed was deafening. I couldn't say the word. Nothing came out of my mouth. I'm sure I looked like a deer caught in headlights. I pulled my Yankees cap over my face and slouched deeper into that oversized couch. I'd worn my hat to every session so far, just for that reason alone. To hide. I looked down at my leg again. It was still shaking. And it was getting on my nerves. So I slapped my hand on my knee to stop it.

"It's ok if you can't say the word. Do you think you can write it down on a piece of paper?" she asked expectantly.

"Sure." It was barely a whisper.

She heard me, though. She passed me a blank piece of paper and a pen.

"Take your time. No rush."

I stared for a moment at this blank page. It felt like an eternity, but I'm sure it was only seconds. Katherine stood up suddenly, pulling a random book from her bookshelf. She then went ahead and opened the book to an equally random page.

"I'll put your piece of paper in this book. This is where it will stay. It doesn't leave this office. It will always be safe here... in this book."

With this reassurance, I finally started printing each letter with more force than was necessary...

RAPE

I literally threw the paper at her and sat back on the couch with my arms crossed. I felt angry having to write that word.

Then Katherine said something that I'd been dying to hear for so long...

"You are not alone, Sydney. Not anymore."

Tears of relief rolled down my cheeks as I began to weep. Finally.

...

Healing

This story is about one person, one woman. At two very different times in her life.

The shy, unsure, twenty-year-old girl, who became captivated with the thought of policing as a career. The very moment she saw a young female officer walk into the café that day, the seed was planted. Followed by a tragic event on that same night, the worst night of her life. An event that would forever change her.

The confident forty-six-year-old woman, who overcame years of self-doubt due to the actions and words of one insignificant human. A woman who finally found the courage to go after what she thought was her dream. Only to have the doubt seep back into her veins. That shy, unsure, twenty-year-old, slowly taking the place of that confident woman.

And his voice, that terrible voice, becoming a thing of nightmares. Again.

"You're ugly. You're stupid. Go kill yourself."

You *will* hear many voices. It can't be avoided. It's part of life. Part of living. Confusing you, convincing you. Telling you how you should feel, act, and respond in life. The negative ones, the internal ones, the external ones in the form of family and friends and everyone in between, the party poopers, the jealous ones, the armchair critics, and the monsters. Ignore every single one of them. Walk through the smoke screen and set your crosshairs on that one voice. The *only* voice you should be listening to is the positive one inside your head. The cheerleader who is rooting for you and has been rooting for you since you emerged into this amazing, sometimes cruel world. Your positive voice is the only one that matters. Believe that voice.

What I have learned is that you can receive all the compliments, pat on the backs, acknowledgements the world has to offer... but if you don't truly believe it, that's exactly what they are: just words. Don't get me wrong; it's nice to hear them. Most people like compliments. I hate them. I still have trouble accepting a nice comment. If someone were to walk up to me right now and tell me they thought I looked beautiful, like my husband often does, my negative inner voice would straight-arm my positive voice out of the way, scoff, and convince me otherwise. Because way back in time, on *that* night, I was told I was ugly and stupid. Well then, it must be true. So I have felt ugly and stupid from that day on. Something I have struggled with internally for years.

Ultimately you are in control of every thought, every voice within. You get to decide how you live, how you respond, what dreams to go after, what thoughts that get to take up space, what to believe in. So believe in you. It's all you. That's a special superpower, in my opinion. Make your thoughts positive and make them count. It is probably one of the most important, if not *the* most important tool on your tool belt. Use it. Filter out the negative voices that life is throwing at you. Pretend you are Captain America. Put that shield up and let all the external bullets, arrows, and insults bounce right off. As for the negative voices in your head... you are Hulk... Hulk smash! So, to that awful external voice that told me I was stupid and ugly on that night so long ago, and to the internal voice inside my head for all these years, convincing me of this: I have no room for you anymore. Take a hike. Let me show you the way out. Better yet, I'll throw you out myself. But not before I smash you into a million pieces. What was that? I can't hear you anymore...

The memory of that awful night came crashing back like it happened yesterday. A slap in the face. Like how dare you try to forget it ever happened? I still control you. It came back at the most inopportune time... at the start of police training.

I don't regret the decision of trying to be a police officer. It has always been something I wanted to do. To work in the community. To help people. I owed it to my younger self. No regrets. I endured twenty weeks of a mentally and physically tough training program. I gave it everything I had. Literally blood, sweat, and tears. Lots of tears. Only to come to the realization that what the job entailed didn't match my personality. I'd have to change for it, something I wasn't willing to do. Policing isn't for everybody. It takes a special person to do the job they do. God bless every single first responder out there. It's a tough gig, and they sacrifice a lot.

I ended my journey just short of graduation. It was one of the hardest decisions I've ever had to make. The mental struggles I was going through from my past trauma, combined with the realization that this job was not for me, were both huge factors contributing to that final decision. The flashbacks of my trauma came at me with a vengeance during my training - memories that I thought had been neatly tucked away, out of sight and out of mind. But memories never really do go away. They can sneak up on you at the most unexpected times...

The entire experience took a heavy toll on me. It has taken time to recover, but I reached out for professional help. I also reached out to my loved ones. Now looking back, I see this chapter for what it was. It was a huge accomplishment. Not a failure in the least. It would have been a failure if I didn't try. My boys had the opportunity to witness their mom put her mind to something and just go for it. To defeat all odds and make a dream a reality. They also had the opportunity to witness their mom crash and burn, the flames to be seen for miles, I'm sure. And then pick herself up and start again. That's where the real lesson in life lies. Now that the dust has settled, I can be proud of my journey. I learned so much about myself and how strong I truly am. From that young girl so many years ago, to the woman I am today... the difference between the two? Astonishing, to say the least. But all the versions necessary for me to be the kind, empathetic, and caring person I am today.

I realize now that a job does not define who I am. The person I am does. That is what I'll be remembered for. My aura, vibe, and how I made people feel... that will be my lasting impression on this earth. I've always wanted to have a career where I can help people. I've chased it my entire life it seems. Helping is in my DNA. But there are many ways to help. It doesn't have to be in the form of any job. Being kind is a good place to start. Sharing your light, your empathy. We all have this innate ability. That is another superpower on our tool belt.

As for the trauma I endured, it was my choice to hold onto this burden for so many years. There is no blame on anyone for this choice. I did the best I could to survive. That's all I could really ask of myself at the time. Most sexual assault victims do not shout it out from a rooftop the second it's over. Some eventually report it. How quickly or slowly after the actual event is irrelevant. Some never say a word about it. There are many valid reasons, factors for the choice you make. Do not ever feel the need to defend whatever decision you make. To anyone. It's your decision. And it's the right decision for you at the time. You do what you can do to survive. My hope is that you do reach out to someone, anyone, and begin the journey of healing. You deserve peace. You deserve a life of happiness. It's a hard step to take, but I promise you it is worth it.

For me, the weight of this burden became heavier with time. It's a hard one to carry all by yourself. Here I am, now choosing to share it with anyone who will take the time to read this. Funny how life has a way of working out. Pick your pain. I could have continued to sit with this, never telling a single soul. It's what I'd sworn to myself: to not tell anyone, no matter what. The shame and embarrassment were walls that kept me from reaching out. So, I sat in this pain for years. Alone. By not sharing my story, I would have continued like this. Struggling to keep my head above water. The difference now? I am no longer ashamed of what happened to me. I now know it was not my fault. I am now choosing to share my story in the hopes of just helping one person.... just one. That is worth it to me. I still feel the pain. It will always be there. But I feel it just a little bit less... and a little bit differently. It's not the hopeless pain I was feeling before. Pick your pain. Choose wisely.

It has been extremely difficult for me to get to this point of forgiveness and moving on. Even writing this was a hard thing for me to do. I won't pretend it was an easy task. Forgiving is hard. And I'm still working on it. I don't know if I will ever forgive the man who ripped the innocence from that young girl. But forgiveness starts somewhere. I first had to learn to accept and forgive that younger version of me...

My Girl

My girl,

My dear, sweet girl.

I'm so sorry I chose to walk away.

From that young woman who needed someone so desperately,

All those years ago.

I chose to not hear your cries for help.

I didn't want anything to do with you.

I hated you.

I was ashamed,

And embarrassed by you.

So, I locked you in a box,

And dumped you into the deepest part of that lake.

You tried to scream, kick, punch your way out.

But I just attached an anchor so you could sink deeper into the back of my mind.

Out of existence… for the time being.

Out of my memory.

If I forgot that it happened, did it ever really happen at all?

Memories never go away.

They may fade over time.

So, I put all my energy into others,

To avoid helping the one person who needed it the most.

That twenty-year-old girl.

Your voice came back in whispers at first,

But slowly turned into screams again.

This time not to be ignored.

That box finally floated to the surface.

The memory crashing back like it happened yesterday.

I will listen to what you have to say this time.

I will really listen.

I forgive you.

I forgive that young woman who didn't know any better.

The girl who only knew how to survive at the time.

Everything will be ok.

I will speak to you going forward,

Like you are my own daughter.

I will give you the love you so desperately need.

And thank you,

For forgiving me,

My present-day self.

For taking this long to let you speak and be heard.

Did I ever mention how stubborn I am?

I will hug you tight.

I won't let you go.

This healing journey will always be a road I will be travelling on,

But this time I will walk down it... hand in hand...

With the girl who just needed to be loved.

Heroes

To the young girl who just wanted to be heard: I hear you now. And I'm so thankful you did not quit on me. You are beautiful, strong, and worthy of love. You are my biggest hero. Thank you for being you. You will always be a part of me.

To the woman I am today... a hero. I don't need a badge to be one. I never did.

My husband... my saviour. You unknowingly rescued a young woman from despair. Simply by offering your hand and a kindness like no other, behind those warm, golden-brown eyes, your love and patience carrying me through. Even after finally finding the courage to tell you my secret... all these years later... your love for me never wavered. Not for a second. It only intensified. You are my hero.

To my boys who needed their mom at times but let me find my way instead. The understanding and grace you have shown me, I will forever be grateful for. I hope you are proud of how far I've come. I know I'm beyond proud of the two amazing humans I am blessed to call my sons.

Sometimes we need a kick in the ass in the form of a beautiful, red-headed therapist to tell us what we are supposed to do next. Some of us need a road map. I needed a well-drawn-out one. You did this for me, Katherine. I will forever hold you dear to my heart. You literally saved me from myself. You inspired me to look deep within myself and find that lost girl. You inspired me to express myself through my writing. You are my hero. You get a green cape. It would look amazing on you.

To my family and friends who have stuck by my side and have seen me at my worst... thank you. You know who you are. I love you. Navigating through this healing journey can be an ugly and messy ride. And you've seen it all. You are my heroes.

To all the amazing women I have met in group therapy... I am in awe of your bravery and courage. Truly. I am blessed to go down this healing journey with you. We share an unbreakable bond. If it took what happened to me for our paths to cross, I say it was worth it. You are all my heroes.

John Roberts... your artwork is astounding. Your beautiful illustration captured the essence of my story. A woman reaching into that lake to help the young girl that was left behind and forgotten about, so long ago. You had me in tears. I will forever be grateful for your artistic wizardry. You are a master at your craft. Thank you, a million times over. You are my hero.

Harley...my six-pound furball of love...thank you for being my sidekick. You stayed with me on the days I struggled to even get out of bed. You celebrated my small victories, when I found enough strength to just go for that much needed walk. I wish all humans can think how dogs do. With unconditional love. You are my hero.

Speaking of heroes...

I finally realized something. My light switch finally turned on. We are all heroes. I will repeat this last statement in bold lettering.

WE ARE ALL HEROES.

If you are struggling mentally or physically, but somehow managed to get out of bed... you are a hero.

If you have lost a loved one and are learning to live life without them... you are a hero.

If you are an exhausted parent who somehow managed to gather enough energy to cook a quick supper... you are a hero. It doesn't have to be gourmet. Kids have survived on Kraft dinner since the beginning of time. Life can be a grind. Keep plugging away.

If you have ever taken the time to strike up a conversation with the convenience store clerk, smile at them, say thank you, make their morning, make them feel important... you are a hero. If you are kind to anyone in any way... boom... hero material right there.

If you feel like you are just floating through life, lost and confused... you are a hero. You may not feel like one at this very moment, but trust me when I say you are to someone. Just for existing in this beautiful and cruel world.

You—reading this right now—you are my hero.

The list goes on. Life can be so wonderful, yet so hard. And we do the best we can.

WE ARE ALL HEROES.

One more thing that my red-headed angel told me: wear that hero cape, tie it on tight, and never let it fall off.

Cindy Henkelman is a first-time author. *Hero Cape* was inspired by her healing journey through therapy. It was her psychologist, Katherine, who planted the seed of writing as a way of healing. This is a story of finding the courage to reach out for help. It is also a story that hopefully resonates with survivors of trauma to help them know they are not alone.

Cindy was born and raised by her parents in Edmonton, Alberta. She is a triplet, having one identical sister and one fraternal sister, as well as an older brother. Her love for her family is never-ending.

Cindy is married to her supportive husband, and they share two wonderful sons together. They currently live in the hamlet of Sherwood Park, Alberta.

Her hobbies include camping, walks with her puppy Harley, working out, reading, connecting with loved ones, and writing. Her biggest passion: meeting new people and hearing their stories.

www.ingramcontent.com/pod-product-compliance
Lightning Source LLC
Chambersburg PA
CBHW051346020726
47501CB00007B/2306